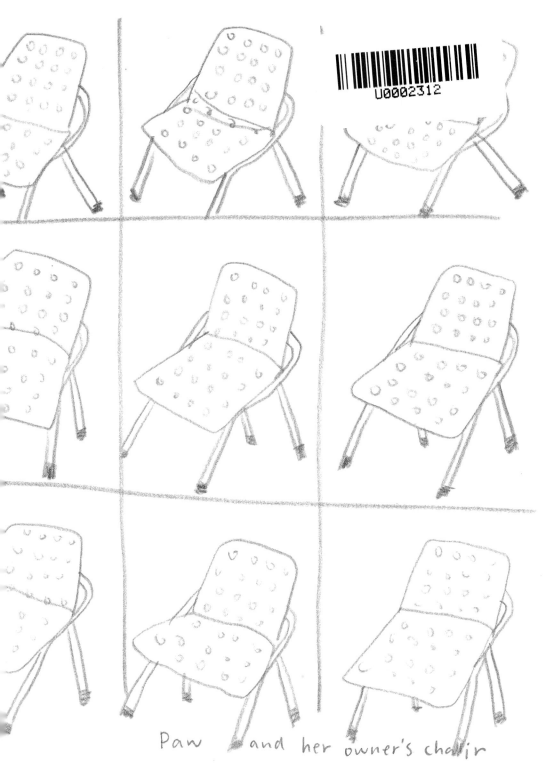

U0002312

Paw and her owner's chair

catch092 Paw in the Surgery

Chinlun Lee (李瑾倫)　文圖

責任編輯：韓秀玫　　美術編輯：何萍萍

法律顧問：全理法律事務所董安丹律師
出版者：大塊文化出版股份有限公司
台北市105南京東路四段25號11樓
讀者服務專線：0800-006689
TEL：(02) 87123898　FAX：(02) 87123897
郵撥帳號：18955675　戶名：大塊文化出版股份有限公司
e-mail:locus@locuspublishing.com
http://www.locuspublishing.com

行政院新聞局局版北市業字第706號
版權所有　翻印必究
總經銷：大和書報圖書股份有限公司　　地址：台北縣五股工業區五工五路2號
TEL：(02) 89902588 (代表號)　FAX：(02) 22901658

初版一刷：2005年5月
定價：新台幣250元
ISBN：986-7291-33-6
Printed in Taiwan

For Eternal Days

Paw in the Surgery

chinlun Lee

I am Paw.

door mat

fan →

A toy from my owner's last

ENTRANCE

My owner here as a

A plant by

(male dogs)

some pet food for sale →

(male dogs)

The pee space of some badly behaved dogs

(male dogs)

weighing scale →

(male dogs)

(female dogs)

(male dogs)

medicine shelves →

Normally, my owner stands here talking to his patients and their owners.

2

X-ray light box

← drip hanger

telephone

medicine tray

another patient's table

dog.
out it
memory.
donated
a customer.

This is a map of our surgery

WINDOW

4 chairs for patients
and their owners
waiting

A filing cabinet
(taller than me)
and my beef snack

A chair that
belongs to my
owner and me.

unknown
mysterious
machine
1

(male dogs)

This is me, Paw.

mysterious
machine
3

machine
4

machine
5

A corridor
towards the
operating
theatre and
patient's room.

He is my owner.

Fortunately and
unfortunately,
he is a vet.

It is very convenient
living in an
animal surgery.

I have my hair
brushed everyday
in the morning
and evening .

I have my
ears cleaned
every three
days.

I am washed
every seven days.

I have the tartar removed from my teeth every one hundred and eighty days.

I am given a vaccination every three hundred and sisty five days.

Normally, I have a

in a primary school's

I would like to

But, sometimes

the walk.

late evening walk
play ground .
do this more often.

he skips

'Too busy today, you know' usually he says. He trys to make me feel better.

He asks me, 'Paw, do you want some milk?'

So, I drink the

milk.

Of course I know
how busy the animal
surgery is.

I am there everyday.

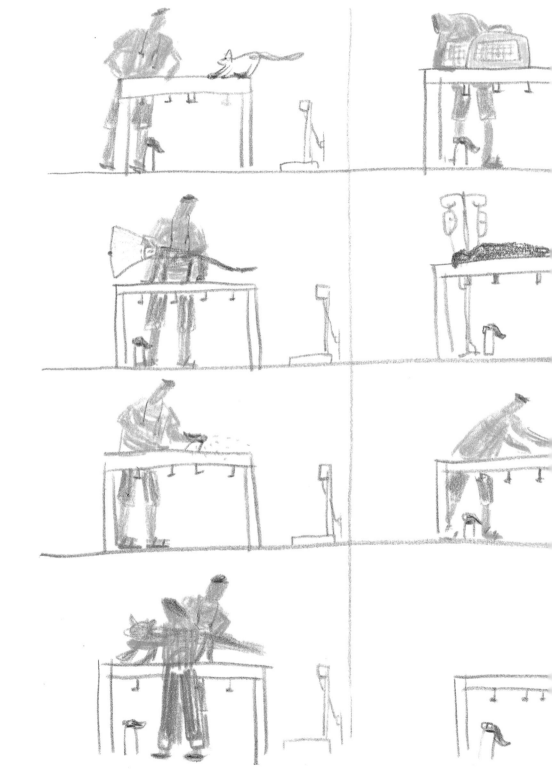